Tug!

Written and illustrated by Matt Buckingham

Collins

Sam picks it up.

2

Tom picks it up.

3

Tim rams it.

Tom rams it.

5

Tom got Sam to tug.

Tom got Tim to tug.

7

Sam runs and tugs.

8

Tim tugs and runs.

9

Tom sits in the sun.

Sam and Tim tug and tug!

11

Sam and Tim sit in the mud.

Tom can tug!

13

Tim and Sam tug